D0952615

L. urents:

Congratulations! Your child is taking the first steps on an exciting journey. The destination? Independent reading!

STEP INTO READING® will help your child get there. The program offers five steps to reading success. Each step includes fun stories and colorful art or photographs. In addition to original fiction and books with favorite characters, there are Step into Reading Non-Fiction Readers, Phonics Readers and Boxed Sets, Sticker Readers, and Comic Readers—a complete literacy program with something to interest every child.

Learning to Read, Step by Step!

Ready to Read   Preschool–Kindergarten
• big type and easy words • rhyme and rhythm • picture clues
For children who know the alphabet and are eager to begin reading.

Reading with Help   Preschool–Grade 1
• basic vocabulary • short sentences • simple stories
For children who recognize familiar words and sound out new words with help.

Reading on Your Own   Grades 1–3
• engaging characters • easy-to-follow plots • popular topics
For children who are ready to read on their own.

Reading Paragraphs   Grades 2–3
• challenging vocabulary • short paragraphs • exciting stories
For newly independent readers who read simple sentences with confidence.

Ready for Chapters   Grades 2–4
• chapters • longer paragraphs • full-color art
For children who want to take the plunge into chapter books but still like colorful pictures.

STEP INTO READING® is designed to give every child a successful reading experience. The grade levels are only guides; children will progress through the steps at their own speed, developing confidence in their reading.

Remember, a lifetime love of reading starts with a single step!

Step into Reading, Random House, and the Random House colophon are registered trademarks of Penguin Random House LLC.

Visit us on the Web!
StepIntoReading.com
rhcbooks.com

Educators and librarians, for a variety of teaching tools, visit us at RHTeachersLibrarians.com

ISBN 978-0-7364-4013-4 (trade) — ISBN 978-0-7364-8282-0 (lib. bdg.)
ISBN 978-0-7364-4014-1 (ebook)

Printed in the United States of America

10 9 8 7 6 5 4 3 2

THE LION KING
Nala and Simba

by Mary Tillworth

illustrated by the Disney Storybook Art Team

Random House 🏠 New York

One morning,
Nala the lion cub
gets a bath.
She sees her best friend,
Simba.

He asks her to play.

Nala and Simba live
on Pride Rock.

They play and run
across the plains.

Zebras salute Simba.

Simba is the son

of King Mufasa.

He will be king one day.

Simba tells Nala

he cannot wait!

Nala and Simba
get lost far from home.

Hyenas find them.

The hyenas are mean.

They trap the cubs.

Nala hears a roar.

It is Mufasa!

He stops the hyenas.

He saves the cubs.

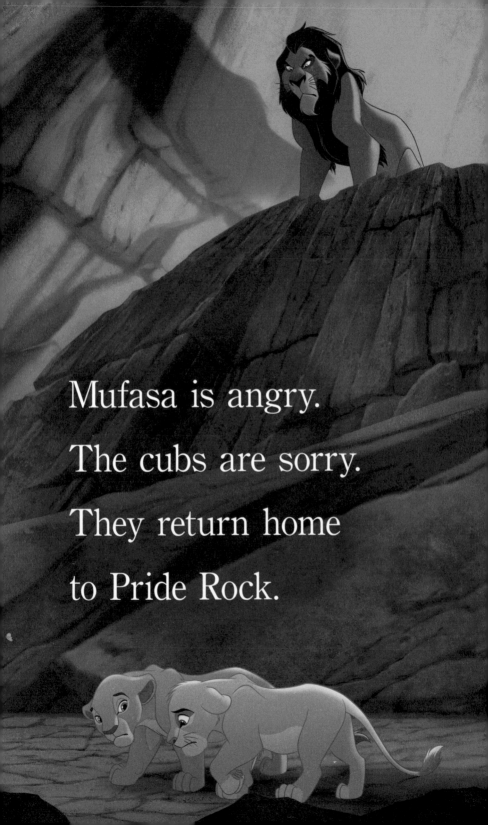

Mufasa is angry.
The cubs are sorry.
They return home
to Pride Rock.

Later,
Simba's uncle Scar
tricks Simba.
Simba thinks he hurt
his father.

Simba runs away.

Scar is now king.

Nala grows up.

She misses Simba.

One day,

she goes hunting

far from home.

A lion attacks her.

Nala pins him down.

It is Simba!

Nala and Simba play.

They fall in love.

Nala tells Simba

to come home.

Nala shows Simba
Pride Rock.

Without a good king,
the land is dry and bare.

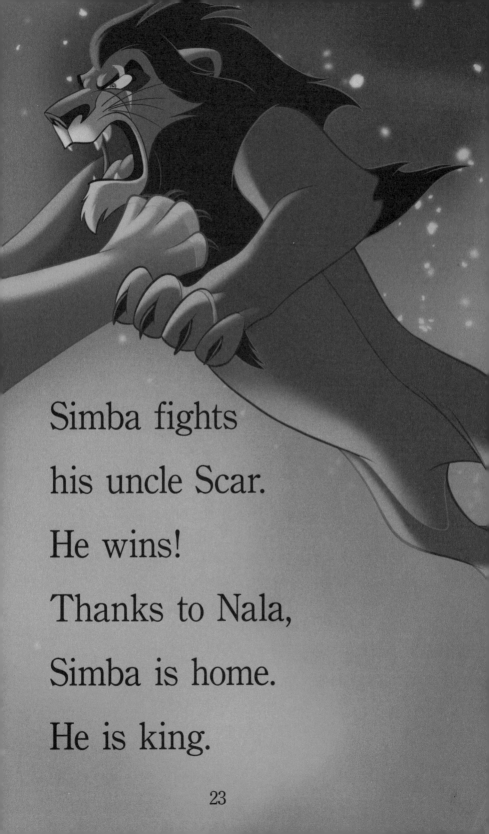

Simba fights
his uncle Scar.
He wins!
Thanks to Nala,
Simba is home.
He is king.

Nala and Simba
rule over Pride Rock.
Nala is a good queen.
Soon they have a cub
of their own!